FLOATING NOTES

Tyrant Books
9 Clinton St
Upper North Store
NY, NY 10002

Via Piagge Marine 23
Sezze (LT) 04018
Italy

www.NYTyrant.com

ISBN 978-0-9992186-1-7

Cover design by Brent Bates
Book design by Adam Robinson

FLOATING NOTES

Babak Lakghomi

tyrant
books

For Sara

I don't remember the first time I wrote my name. What I do remember is the first time someone else was called my name. I told him that was my name, too, but he couldn't believe it. He was a fat boy with a puffy face. He looked like a little boxer.

Now, people call me in different names and I don't care. Why people call me other names might be because I am not writing my name the right way, though that is how it's written in my documents. Foreheads furrow whenever I say my name, and I have to take my papers out and show them to see for themselves.

I sometimes introduce myself as Bob, but only where I am sure nobody knows me. I have to be careful or they would know I'm not Bob.

Coffee shops are among the places that I call myself Bob. I sometimes forget I am Bob and my coffee grows cold. I never go twice to the same coffee shop.

Where is this name from? This is the question that I have to answer whenever I say my real name. Cab drivers, clerks. I rarely take a cab. Then they tell me they have a friend who has the same name. I think about all the people in the world with my name and their cab driver friends.

I don't have friends, and the only one that I had was not a cab driver or a clerk. My name became a different name in her mouth. I want to say I loved hearing it from her and maybe I did, but any time I heard it, I feared I had done something wrong.

I wonder how the fat boy writes his name, and if he, like me, is being called different names.

My name is Bob, and this is what I call my life: an attic room with a yellow curtain in a narrow hallway, a spring bed on the creaking floor. Notebooks in a knapsack. Two cups of coffee per day.

The walls of my room are thin. A French man lives in the room next to me. His bed leans on the shared wall and I sometimes hear him cry at night. Sometimes women are over and I hear them through the thin wall too. The French man says he has been a pilot in France, but I don't believe him.

This is my life after I left, or after she left me and I decided to leave, too.

My landlord is a Chinese woman. She has turned one of the rooms in the hallway into a shop where she sells plastic plants. You wonder how many people would buy plastic plants, but the hallway is always full.

In the hallway, there is a shared kitchen and a bathroom with two stalls. In the kitchen, a fridge is filled with food with name tags. I put my eggs and fruits in the fridge. I keep my bread in the drawer by the side of my bed. My eggs always go missing from the fridge, even though they have tags. I think this might have something to do with the French man.

The good thing is the eggs can be easily replaced. The room is in the same building with a Chinese grocery store. Fruits are stacked in the front section of the store. The back part places fresh fish, clams, live lobsters. I like watching the lobsters in the buckets, smelling the smell of sea.

My father had a small boat back home, we fished from the river there. Here, I fished on a large boat on the ocean. I remember the sound of the gulls fishing for the guts of fish that we threw back into the ocean. The smell of blood and salt. I gutted thousands of fish per day, my boots deep into the cold water. The blood from the boat left a red trail on the sea.

I found an office job after. I also started writing again—articles that I sent to different journals. You don't believe me? I have them here in my knapsack. But I couldn't publish them under my own name.

I threw all of my books in the river before I left the country. This was the same river that my father used to fish.

Let's say the office job wasn't for me either. I always had my notebook open beneath the work folders. My stomach turned when they called my name. I was always waiting for a Monday morning when my boss would ask me to his office. All I remember from that place is the toilet. Spreading toilet paper on the seat, flushing multiple times, drinking from my flask. The boss started to follow me to the toilet door and wait there until I was done.

When I don't know where else to go I like to go to the abandoned water treatment plant. From the hill there, I can watch the ocean. I don't remember when I went there for the first time. The grass was tall, and the wind moved the branches of the birch trees. The gulls called, and you could still hear the plant pumps. The place used to remind me of a hill we used to hike to with my wife. She hadn't been my wife then. It was a place we went to when we didn't know where else to go. The city beneath us, we watched the city through the clouds. Years later, in a visit back, I went there and the place had turned into a dumpster. Dust, rusted metal, syringes. Dried grass.

Here, you can still hear the gulls and the waves crashing against the cliffs and rusted pumps. The doors of the plant building are locked now. I once tried to open one of the doors with a screw driver. But I think I need different tools. Next time, I'll bring in pliers, wrench, a small hand saw, hammer.

I had a photo of her until a while ago. It was the only photo I'd recovered from that negative. It was in my old wallet in the bedside table where I also kept my bread. The wallet had been there until two days ago.

I pulled the curtains and looked outside at the street from the narrow gap between the window frame and the curtain. A black car stopped next to the massage parlor. I put my ear on the wall to see if the French man was home, but I couldn't hear anything. I looked out from the peephole. Two men with beards left the room with plastic plants in a box. I hadn't seen any men buying plastic plants before.

I went to the corner of the room where I had my toolbox on a shelf. I opened the toolbox, but instead of the tools I was looking for I found my father's gutting knife. I didn't know how my father's gutting knife had ended up there. I didn't remember seeing it since I'd left the fishing boat and found the job at the office. The hammer and hand saw were still there, but the pliers and wrench were missing. I took the hammer and saw from the toolbox and put them in my knapsack. I left my father's gutting knife where it was.

She was my wife when she asked me not to leave the house. We had a three-year-old son then. She said she had seen a black car on the street. I looked out the window and showed her the empty street. But she didn't believe me. She took my father's knife from the kitchen and put its edge on her wrist. She pressed the tip on her pale skin. I grabbed her by her wrists and twisted her arms. She didn't drop the knife.

I pushed her on the floor and fell on top of her.

A sharp pain pointed to my armpit. My blood stained her summer dress.

Our son was watching this.

I didn't go to meet the contact that day. I stayed home for a week. After that, we took my father's truck and loaded all my books and notebooks into the trunk. I drove the truck to the river, down to my father's boat.

Two days later a black car stopped by our house when she was at work. Two men came in to search the house. They emptied all the drawers and shelves into plastic bins. I wasn't sure if they were looking for the notebooks or not, but whatever they were looking for, they couldn't find it.

They duct-taped my eyes and took me to the car. I don't know where I was taken. They locked me in a cell that I suspected was in a garden. I could smell the soil, pine, and walnut trees. A horse neighed in the garden.

When I came back home, my son's toys were still on the floor. My wife's clothes had collected dust in the closet.

I put my ear on the wall to the sound of somebody in the next room. The French man was not usually in the room at this time of the day. I watched the hallway through the peephole and waited for him to leave. I listened and when I didn't hear anything, I took a piece of wire and went to the hallway, my heart flapping against my chest. I knocked at the French man's door, inserted the wire into the lock, and twisted it until I heard the click.

In the room, separated by our shared wall, there was a bed near my bed. In the corner of the room, cartons of eggs were stacked on the shelves. A camera on a tripod was pointed at the eggs. I opened different drawers and couldn't find any sign of my lost wallet. Instead, I found multiple photos of eggs, a pilot certificate in French. The photo on the certificate had no resemblance to my neighbour. When I heard footsteps, I put the certificate in my back pocket. I left the room.

Outside, women were entering the room with plastic plants.

She asked me if we had printed the photos and I told her that the negative was over-exposed. I don't remember if I said over-exposed or lost. I don't think I would have known what over-exposed was then, but I might have just repeated what my father said. All I remember is that it was my birthday and my father had asked for her parent's permission to take her with us on his boat. The camera was my uncle's camera. Maybe my father didn't know how to work with the camera and that was why what happened did.

We swam in the river and watched the birds: storks, white egrets, cranes. My father stopped the motor and paddled to a place where the seagulls had laid their eggs. He took photos of the two of us on his boat on the river. Me and her. Our arms on each other's backs.

When I don't know what else to do I like to write down things in my notebook. I like to do this in a laundromat or a coffee shop. I sit by the window and write. I sometimes cut pieces from newspapers and attach them to the pages.

Some of the notebooks were thrown into the river. Some of them were lost in a flood.

Now, I write my notes in a very small handwriting that only I can read.

Some nights I dream I am on my father's boat and I'm fishing my old notebooks from the bottom of the river.

When I saw the French man in the hallway, his front tooth was cracked. He had a bruise under his left eye. This didn't make him look more like the photo in the certificate. I waited for him to leave his room and I followed him when he did. I was prepared to follow him for a long time, but as he left the building he entered the massage parlor. I waited there for a while and then I entered the massage parlor, too.

There was a golden statue of a paw-waving cat on a table. A door opened and a young woman came out in a short white outfit.

Want some massage?

I didn't know what to do to not make her suspicious.

Twenty for twenty, she said.

I fished into my pocket to take out the bills that I have, but instead I took out the pilot certificate. I could see her eyes lock into the picture before I put it back.

I'll come back later, I said.

She pushed on a bell beside the cat statue and a bulky bald man came out in a suit.

You need something? The man's belly was about to burst the buttons of his shirt.

I took the bill this time and put it on the table. Just a massage, I said.

The woman took the bill and directed me into a long hallway.

A white leather bed in a dim room. The smell of oil and candles. The sound of waves crashing against the cliffs. I closed my eyes. I liked skin on my skin. The price changed depending on how far the hands traveled. My hands stayed at the borders. I didn't want to risk passing the border without permission. Even the borders were plump like a peach. I was happy staying at the borders. I could feel the heat there. Hard against soft. The boat rocking against the waves.

On the wall, a set of screens showed the hallway, the front entry. I heard a bell ring and watched a man enter the massage parlor. The woman left me on the bed, handing me a wet warm towel.

On the screen, I saw the man and the woman enter another room. When the door opened, I could see two other men sitting on opposite chairs in the room. One of them was tied to his chair.

Some nights I wake up and hear a horse neighing.

I know you called me Bob, but that's not my name, Lily. But if you want to call me Bob, that is okay, too. You had brown eyes, flat collarbone, a fine neck. You asked me what I was writing, and I didn't know what to call it.

I didn't know if it was your mouth, or the color of your skin that made me think of birds.

Do you like birds?

Birds?

Yes. Birds.

I asked you if you wanted to go to a wastewater treatment plant to watch birds, and you laughed. There was something beautiful about your laughter though you didn't want to go to the wastewater treatment plant. I didn't want to insist. Instead, we decided to go to the zoo.

The veins beneath your skin: the roads on my map.

If you follow them, you won't get lost, you said.

When I looked out the window of my apartment, I saw that the black car had stopped by the massage parlor again. I couldn't hear anything from the next room or see any light through its window. The French man hadn't returned to his place.

To go back to the French man's place would've been falling straight into their trap. They were probably watching the hallways, too.

If I didn't do anything, after a while they would leave me to myself.

I looked at my map. There was a phone number on the top corner. I showed her the map when we got off the bus, trying to tell her that we were not at the right place. I didn't know when she'd written down her number on the map.

She took my hands and led me to a trail into the woods. Did she know that we weren't going to the zoo from the beginning? It seemed she was comfortable not knowing where we were going. I liked that.

The woodpeckers drummed the dead sycamore trees. The wind moved strands of her hair. She piled them away from her face. I still had the map folded in my hand when she grabbed it from me and dropped it on the leaves. She pushed me against an aspen tree, pressed the palms of her hands on my chest, looked into my eyes.

Dew sat on the orange leaves beneath our boots.

We kissed.

The taste of her mouth: rinds of lemon, forests of mountain trees, a Bach cello suite. Her tongue: the cave of forgotten dreams.

She grabbed my hand again. She started running in the trail.

In the bus, I talked about the birds and fish in our river. She smiled at me, holding my hand, but then became silent.

The sun was going down. We both stared outside at the long shadows of the trees, the falling light in the red sky.

See you tomorrow at the coffee shop, she said when we were leaving the bus station.

She kissed me on the cheek.

I didn't tell her that I can't go to the same coffee shop again.

I looked for my wife and son after they left me. Everybody tried to hide it from me where they were. My wife's parents didn't answer my calls. The neighbours whispered things when they saw me on the street. For most of the day, I lied on the bed with the TV on, forking my food from a can.

They had taken everything in the bins: my passport, my driver's license, photos, letters. The rest, I had thrown in the river myself.

I put on my wife's shirts, wore her perfume.

One day, my sister-in-law knocked at my door.

I let her in.

She told me that I needed to let it go. That I deserved better. She held my hand as she told me this. Move on is what she said.

Her hands were smaller than Ava's. She had similar curly hair and long eyelashes, but her skin wasn't as dark.

Ava is married to someone else, she told me.

Where is Ava? I asked.

She said, I cannot tell you that.

She said, I did this for you.

She said, No one should know that I was here.

In order to use the phone you had to go to the room with the plastic plants. At night, nobody was in the room. Still, I looked around to make sure I wasn't being watched, though there wasn't a way to know if your voice was being recorded.

I dialled the number, but nobody responded. A voice recording told me to leave my message. I wasn't sure if the voice was hers. It didn't resemble her voice, but voices sound different on the phone, and who knows, maybe she had a roommate. I didn't know that much about her life after all.

What if my only chance to see her had been going to the coffee shop the day after our day in the woods?

I left a message.

It's Bob from the coffee shop. Sorry I didn't show up the other day. I was so happy to find your phone number. Do you want to go to the trail again, or the zoo? I'll be at the bus station on Wednesday morning at ten.

Her name was Lily, or that was the name she introduced herself with.

Bob and Lily, I thought.

After I left the message, I asked, What if she doesn't hear the message and we never see each other again?

I was in these thoughts when I saw a silhouette moving in front of me. The silhouette reached closer, something like a rifle in his hand.

Mister, what are you doing this time of the night?

It was only the landlord.

I couldn't believe that they had left the negative in the camera behind, that it wasn't taken away in one of the bins. The negative was the only sign of our five years together. When I printed the negative, all of the photos were over-exposed, except that one.

It wasn't the first time this was happening to me.

In the photo, she was sitting in front of a wall that we had painted blue. The light from the window made the curls of her hair look lighter. Her head was tilted towards our son on her lap.

How could I lose the only photo that I had recovered from the negative? The only photo that connected me to them, to this previous life.

Now, they had that photo, and I had a pilot certificate in French.

I was reading an old newspaper in the laundromat when I saw his name. The name of the dead man was the same as the name of the contact. I'd been supposed to see the contact on the day that my wife didn't let me leave the house.

The contact's body had been found on the shores of the ocean in a foreign city where he'd travelled for business. Based on the newspaper, local and international police were still looking into the cause of death.

The newspaper in the laundromat was from four months ago, so the police should've resolved the case by now.

I'd always imagined that the contact was arrested and hanged. If he was arrested with all of the documents, he wouldn't have been left alive. If he wasn't arrested, there was no way for them to know about my role.

Now, years later, on another side of the world, I had to ask myself if the contact had been actually hanged at the time.

What if the documents were only recently found? What if that was why he'd been murdered now? Would they come after me again after these many years? They had mercenaries in every corner of the world.

I cut the piece from the newspaper and glued it into my notebook.

I had to go to the public library and look into the archives. It was a short walk from the laundromat to the library. I decided to leave my clothes until they dried and come back after.

No matter how much I enjoyed the smell of dust, of old paper, and of the silence beneath the high ceilings, my visit to the public library wasn't the same trip this time. I looked into the archives of the newspaper, reviewing every single day after the date of the first report. I couldn't find anything. I reviewed other newspapers, too, but that wasn't helpful either.

I wondered if pretending that everything was normal was still the best way. Maybe I had to go somewhere where they couldn't find me.

I remembered that I had left a message to see Lily on Wednesday. How stupid of me to suggest Wednesday instead of today. I couldn't leave without seeing her. But wasn't I putting her into risk by meeting her again?

When I returned to the laundromat, my underwear and shirts were scattered on the floor. An old man was sitting in front of my dryer, solving a crossword puzzle.

After my sister in law's visit, I left the house more. One day, I rode my bike down to the river, my fishing rod on the back basket. I paddled through the reeds, my father's boat on the muddy river.

It was a cool day with a breeze. I stopped the boat in a narrow stream, watched the gulls guarding their eggs. My fishing rod into the river, I heard the roaring of a motor boat. The calling of the gulls became louder. Two men were on the boat with tanned faces and bare hairy chests, wearing loose khaki pants. One of them held a copper cable connected to the motor, the other one held a net.

The first man inserted the bare cable into the water and started the engine. The boat bobbed and dead fish floated to the surface of the water. The birds on the water froze with their wings half open.

The other man collected birds and fish in his net. He separated birds from fish and put them in a separate bucket.

The first man took a cutlass and started skinning the birds. He broke the necks first, and made two cuts into the flesh. With two movements of his hand the skins swiftly came off.

I started to paddle my way out through the floating fish and the calling of gulls attacking dead fish.

On Tuesday morning, I tried to call the number on the map, but I got the voice message again. I decided I would wait until Wednesday before I packed my knapsack and left the attic.

I took my binoculars and tried to look into the massage parlor. The curtains were pulled and you couldn't see anything except the sign "OPEN" on the door. The black car was still parked in front of the massage parlor, but nobody was inside the car. I watched a middle-aged man enter and leave the place.

I wasn't planning to leave the attic room on that day, but when I went to the kitchen, I didn't find any eggs in the fridge. I didn't remember if I had any before and if I had eaten them or if they were stolen again. But who was stealing my eggs if it wasn't the French man? I had seen all the eggs in his room before he disappeared.

I went to the grocery store to get some eggs and I saw the two men with beards there. I pretended that I hadn't noticed them and went to look at the lobsters in the bucket. Looking at the lobsters always helped clear my mind. For a moment, I thought maybe my main lead was the pilot certificate. It had to belong to someone, and if I knew whose it was, that would help me understand what was going on.

When I came back to my room, someone knocked at my door.

It was the landlord again.

Mister, there was a phone call for you.

I thought Lily, and I could feel blood flowing in my veins.

Did she leave a message?

No. No message. No one call you. Only you call. No one call. Okay?

Okay.

I ran to the room with plants to call her, but got the voice message again.

When I was kept at the cell at the garden, every day a miniature door on the bottom of the door opened and a pair of hands pushed a steel food plate inside the cell. Every day, I begged the hands to talk to me: let me know where I was, why I was there.

I begged them to give me paper and books.

One day the mini door opened and on the plate was a pile of paper and a book.

On Wednesday, I went to the bus station and looked for Lily. People moved around the station, their paper cups in their hands. The place smelled of burnt coffee, perfumes, bread. On the bench where we had sat together, a young girl sat with her eyes closed.

I walked around the station, and then went back to where the bench was, but didn't find any sign of Lily. I was standing there, my left eye twitching from sleeplessness when somebody tapped on my shoulder.

Bob? She said.

She was a girl with a bony face, short black hair, and a big glasses frame. Beneath the glasses, she had small blue eyes.

This is Sheila. I am Lily's roommate. I got your voice messages.

Where is Lily? Is she okay?

I thought you might know something about her, Sheila said. She hasn't come back home in the last five days.

It was difficult to trust her. What if she was sent by them? What if they had just heard the phone conversation and had sent her to lead me where they wanted me to be led.

Lily was talking about people following her the day before she disappeared, Sheila said. She also talked about meeting you at the coffee shop. I think you should trust me, Sheila said, and tell me whatever you know.

I don't know why, but I started to.

The house was blue, its door was red. They had a shared living room, one bedroom, a den. The den was separated with a black velvet curtain. In the living room, there was a beige sofa bed, a desk. A painting on the wall behind the sofa. It was too big for the small living space. The portrait looked like Sheila.

I wished the first time I'd gone there was with Lily.

Nice painting, it looks like you, I said.

That's one of Lily's, Sheila said. She painted me.

I didn't know she painted.

You don't know a whole lot about her, do you? She doesn't paint people anymore.

What does she paint?

She paints lame horses.

Are you sure you want me to stay here?

I think so. After what you told me, we'll both feel safer this way. You can sleep on Lily's bed, or on the sofa bed, if you prefer. When we were afraid, Lily and I would sleep together on the sofa bed here.

You seem to be pretty close.

Sheila didn't respond to this and just looked at me from the corner of her eyes.

Lily's bed was a single bed with white sheets and a hand-knitted colorful bed cover. I got into the bed wondering if this was how she smelled.

At night, I woke with the sound of a horse neighing in my head. The wind was moving the black curtain. I could hear someone breathing, could see a pair of white feet beneath the curtain.

Sheila, I called.

The feet moved across the floor.

◎ ◎ ◎

During breakfast, Sheila talked more about Lily, about a period that she had become a nun in the Nepalese mountains. I loved the way Sheila talked when she talked about Lily.

What do you think made her return here?

I don't know. Maybe she was tired of escaping.

I imagined Lily, her head shaved, white cotton wrapped around her. For some reason, I pictured her pregnant. I put my head on her belly.

Sheila held my hand. I didn't talk about what I had seen last night. Maybe I had dreamed it, and if not, then what?

Sheila, I think it will be less risky for you if I stay back at the attic, I said.

But what about you?

I'll be careful.

I think you need to leave the pilot certificate with me.

I agreed.

The book they gave me in the cell was about the birds of the world travelling to find their king. I still had the book below my pillow, although I knew its contents by heart. I wanted to give the book to Lily.

It was in China, late one moonless night,
The Simorgh first appeared to mortal sight –
He let a feather float down through the air,
And rumours of its fame spread everywhere;

I wondered whether I would have to go hide in the water treatment plant, but I was still hopeful that Lily would come back and we could leave together.

I wanted to know Lily more, to know everything about her. I'd found a diary in her room, but reading it would have been unfair without her permission. I wondered whether Sheila had read it. I resisted reading it.

The sun had painted yellow strips on the wall behind my bed. I missed hearing the sound of the French man crying. There was still no sign of him being back. I opened the drawer and took a dry loaf of bread to eat, swallowing it with some water. I think I had gone to sleep, when I heard someone knocking at the door.

When I looked through the peephole, I saw it was the woman from the massage parlor.

Open the door, she kept knocking.

When I didn't, she slid a note in through the door gap.

They're planning to take you down tonight. I happened to overhear them talking. I'll be waiting for you in the back alley with a red car at 5 pm. We don't have time.

Why would she want to help me? I thought about her soft big hands.

She was waiting there at 5 with the red car. She suggested driving me to the border, but then agreed with my suggestion for hiding in the water treatment plant.

I could feel you're different, she said, as I laid my hands on you.

I had everything I needed packed in my knapsack and a small suitcase. I had a sleeping bag, too.

Will you share your bag with me?

I didn't know how that was possible, but I nodded.

We passed corn farms and abandoned factories. She drove slowly and pushed her foot on the brake forcefully when we got close to another car.

Do you know why they're after me?

I think it might have something to do with your neighbour, she said.

Did you tell them about the pilot certificate?

What pilot certificate?

How did you end up working there? Did they force you?

No, she said. I responded to a job ad.

How did you know where I lived?

It wasn't too hard to find out. Relax!

Her right hand slid below my shirt, rubbing my belly, then moved under my pants. Her left hand kept to the steering wheel, eyes on the bumpy road.

The sky was gray. The leaves of the trees had fallen, waiting for snow. I could smell the ocean.

I had to saw off a small door into the entrance door to be able to get into the plant. The building had high ceilings and red brick walls. There were narrow passages between the walls and the pools. Most of the pools were empty, mold covering their walls. The pumps and pipes had rusted, their surfaces flaking.

I suggested staying in the control room. The control room was blue. The paint peeled on its walls. There were still desks in the blue room, a dilapidated sofa, two chairs. The room's big windows were covered with old newspapers. Inside the desk drawers, there were cigarettes, coffee mugs, spoons. Whatever the reason was, people had left the place quickly, leaving their traces everywhere behind them.

I unzipped the sleeping bag and spread it on the floor. I offered her bread from my knapsack. After eating, she took off her pants. We went to sleep with our jackets covering us, our legs rubbed.

The wind howled through the gaps of the window. I could hear waves crash against the cliffs. Her body was warm. It was as close as I had slept to a body after Ava had left.

Every day, we would drive to a small town ten minutes away from the plant where there was a pub and a convenience store. We bought what we needed—cans of food, logs of wood, water, fire starter. I cleaned the control room and made a fire pit, where I made a fire every night. I put the logs into the pit and covered it with old papers. I poured the fire starter on the papers.

Sometimes when I thought about the lost photo or about Lily, a pain would punch me in the chest. I woke up in the middle of the night, looking at the body beside me, unfamiliar, red in the fire light.

I opened Lily's diary and read through it. Her words soothed me, even though they talked about pain.

We were running out of cash, my last welfare check was almost gone. We needed to have a plan. Or maybe we could go back and pick up the check and come back here. I told the woman from the massage parlor I would take the car to do this even though I hadn't driven in years. I wanted to go to Sheila's place and learn more about Lily.

I hadn't told the woman from the massage parlor anything about Lily.

When Lily was five, her mother left them. It was her and her father after, the horses and cows in the barns. Lily passed most of her time in the barn with a pony called Peter. Was she able to ride the pony at that age? I hadn't found anything about that in the notebook. I had never been in a barn myself.

She woke up one night from a bad dream, and went to his father's bedroom, found him passed out on the bed, eyes half-open, a syringe fallen beside him. His throat made noises like a boiling kettle.

Two of their horses died. Lily's father dug their graves on the back of the farm, on a patch of green grass. He tied their bodies to his truck and pulled them on the ground towards the graves.

Lily went to sleep every night with the fear that she'd wake up and find Peter dead in the morning.

When I was inside her, she asked me what I was doing. I was doing what I had been doing before, but my mind was elsewhere.

This happened the same night that I took her to the pub in town to buy her beer. A biker in a black bandana bought her beer, too, and taught her how to play billiards.

When I woke up that night, the fire had turned to ashes. There was no sign of a body beside me. I looked and looked. She had taken my suitcase, the car, the cash left from my last check. She had left my knapsack behind, but Lily's notebook and my suitcase were gone.

I didn't have enough money for a bus fare, so I decided to walk back.

The snow had piled on the road side and it was hard to see the car lights through the fog. The last time I had walked such a long distance was when I heard about the whereabouts of my wife. I never found out if she was actually where I'd heard she was.

Whoever had told me about Ava's whereabouts had also introduced me to the dog-faced man who helped me cross the border. I don't think it was any of my old contacts that introduced me to the dog-faced man, since I would have been too afraid to get in touch with any of them.

The dog-faced man came to meet me in our house in a tight black leather jacket to discuss the details of his plan. I sold whatever was left: my father's boat, the truck, pieces of furniture.

I used most of the money to pay the dog-faced man to pass me through the border.

He hid us inside the tank of a truck. I couldn't breathe. My lungs filled with something thick. Small children coughed and cried. I smelled of gasoline when I got out.

Then, I rode a mule through the snowy mountains on a narrow road to where the dog-faced man had marked on my map. Someone was going to help me when I got to this spot.

After two days of riding, the mule brayed and stopped walking. Its limbs went deeper into the snow. I had to leave it behind and continue on my own. I walked for two days, knee-deep into snow and ice-cold rivers until I got to the point on the map.

When I was a kid, my mother used to take me to the public bath early in the mornings. The cold mornings, the river frozen, asphalt cracked, me and her walked through a tunnel of snow. After the tunnel, I knew the bath was waiting for me, the warmth of the steam, the smell of soap, the female bodies through the fog. My body would go numb with the sudden change of temperature. I soaked myself in the small pool and sat on the big white stone until my mother would rub me with her wash cloth, something growing in the pit of my stomach. I felt like I was falling, not wanting anyone to grab me.

I reached the city at night. The cars sped past me. The snow had turned to rain and I arrived with my clothes soaked. On the streets, it was probably my smell that made people turn. I went inside a drug store, opened a bottle of cough syrup, had two gulps. My chest went warm. I put the bottle back where it was and left the drug store, still shivering from the cold. I couldn't go back to the attic. I didn't know who or what was expecting me there.

In front of a laundromat, I warmed myself with the steam coming out of the curbside sewer and waited until nobody was inside. I went in and undressed, leaving only my underwear on. I ran a wet paper towel all over my body, and placed my dirty clothes into a washer, sat there on the bench. As I was starting the washer, a boy came in his sweatpants to pick up his dried clothes. He opened a drier and threw me a hot towel from it. I rubbed it against my face and became dizzy from the smell.

Do you want a tea or something? He had big brown eyes that looked down on his feet when he talked to me, an accent I couldn't recognize.

I'm fine, I said to him, though I could really use a tea.

I sat there when the boy left. Outside, there weren't many people in the streets. Through the glass, I saw shadows with umbrellas pass in the dim light.

I was starting to feel like myself again.

◎ ◎ ◎

The ministry of labour opened at 9 am. I decided to pass the remaining time at a coffee shop. I still had some change left for a coffee, and it felt good to be back to my routine.

I looked at my map. The ministry was in an area I had been to before. There were several marked points on my map, but in an alley I was able to find a new coffee shop. It seemed like one of those places that only a few regulars knew about. There was an old type writer on a tall table. I was tempted to try to type something on the white paper. When the barista, a young man with a moustache and a pony tail, asked me:

The regular, Bob?

I looked around at the otherwise empty coffee shop. I rushed out the coffee shop, my heart throbbing in my ears.

◎ ◎ ◎

There was a line up in front of the ministry even though I was early. A guard in a black uniform checked the documents of the people in the line. I took out my documents from the knapsack.

What is your request? I don't see any forms attached.

I want to get my last check.

The checks were mailed on the assigned date.

I don't live at the same address anymore.

You need form 401 for the change of address. You can pick it up from two blocks south of here.

I bought a hot dog with my remaining change and walked through a park to the place where you could pick up the form. The birds were pecking at breadcrumbs. Pigeons. Sparrows. Gulls. Baby sitters played with kids at the playground. A man was swinging his son, the little boy was shrieking in excitement.

Every day when I got back from work, I used to put my son in the stroller, go for a long walk in the park. When we got into the playground, he would sit on the bench and watch the other kids. After I persuaded him, he would do one round of "slide and see-saw," then come back and sit on the bench again, staring at birds, kids, dogs. One day I sat on the swing myself holding him tightly and swinging back and forth. Higher, higher, he shrieked. It seemed whatever fear he had had disappeared.

I thought he would be in high school now.

I picked the form from the basement of an old building. But I still needed to somehow get my last check. I wondered whether the landlord had rented my place to someone else, or I could still enter the attic with my old key.

I walked to the Chinese grocery store, studying the area from there. I couldn't see a sign of the black car or the men with beards. The "OPEN" sign flashed on the massage parlor window. Everything seemed to be as it was before any of this had started. I took the back stairs to the hallway, waited behind the door until I could hear no sounds from the hall. I wasn't sure if I should just enter the hallway and try opening the attic door using my old key.

My temples burned from hunger or the thought of all of this. I opened the stairway, took big steps towards the attic, turning my head to check the hallway with every step. After making sure nobody was around, I inserted the key and turned. The door opened.

I fell on the floor. Envelopes surrounded me. One of the envelopes was from the ministry with my check inside it.

There was another envelope with nothing written on the back. When I opened it, I found the pilot certificate inside. Why had Sheila mailed the certificate back to me? She had volunteered to keep it herself.

Everything else in the attic seemed as if it had been left. I opened the drawer. Nothing was inside except the bread covered in mold. My father's gutting knife wasn't in the toolbox. Somebody had been there, but had probably not expected the pilot certificate to be in the envelope.

I heard a door open in the hallway, looked through the peephole, and saw a man leave the French man's room. I looked at the pilot certificate again. The man in the French man's room was the man in the photo.

What had happened to the French man himself?

I didn't turn on the lights, spent the night in the attic in my old bed, putting my ear on the wall.

When I left the attic, it was still dark. My tongue was heavy, my stomach burned. Nobody was in the streets. I had to wait for the bank to open.

Once I cashed the check, I could check into a motel, eat, take a shower.

I had stayed in a motel the first time I arrived in this city. Most of the stores in the street had been abandoned since, the items on displays covered in dust. The motel was one of the few places that had stayed open. The exterior hadn't changed much, still painted in yellow. There were two cars in the parking lot, one of them a police car.

Could I provide the address of the motel for the ministry? Maybe I was better off renting a box in the post office. Of course I had to pay for the box, but it gave me the ability to pick up my check if they found my place and I had to move again.

I remembered the motel room from my first stay there, the radiator making noises at nights, young people screaming in the parking lot. The first couple of days, the room had been cold, and I'd had to sleep with my jacket on.

I looked at the entrance door to the reception and wondered if I should enter. They didn't usually ask for the money up front. There were two tables in the reception area where they served eggs for breakfast. Scrambled was the only way you could get them. Paintings of trees and snowy roads were on the walls. The carpets smelled of mildew.

A policeman in his uniform left one of the rooms. He looked around the empty street and looked at me before getting into his car. I started walking. A woman was walking in front of me, dragging her left foot on the ground, pushing a cart. The wind banged the cans hanging from the cart. When the woman turned into an alley, I was left alone.

The snow had melted. The roots of the trees had cracked the sidewalk. My eyes followed a truck disappear into a garage behind a fence. After the fence, a river with foaming water flowed beneath a bridge.

◉ ◉ ◉

After I cashed my check, I walked back towards the motel. I was so hungry that I went into the first place that seemed to have anything to serve. It was the only place open on the street after I left the bank. Wine glasses hung from a rack. Long stools were placed in front of the counter. The woman behind the counter had the big tattoo of a head of a bird. The tattoo started on her shoulders and disappeared beneath her top. She asked me what I wanted. I asked her what they had, which was only coffee and pastries.

But this place looks like a pub, I said.

Well, it was a pub before. But my husband doesn't want me to serve liquor anymore.

She put a cup of coffee on the counter, a croissant on a white plate. The crust was greasy. I felt the grease curdle in my empty stomach. I washed the grease down with coffee.

There was a shooting here a while ago, the woman said.

Yeah, she said. She stared outside like the scene was recurring in her head. Then she grabbed the coffee pot, refilled my cup.

I imagined the body of the contact floating on the ocean, his face deformed, his skin swollen and green.

Sorry to hear that, I said.

It's not your fault, she said.

I took out my map and marked the place on it, even though it was not really a coffee shop.

On the corner of the place there was a telephone.

Can I use the phone?

Suit yourself.

I dialled the number on the map, but no one picked up.

I went back and sat on my stool.

You seem like you can use a drink, the woman said. She took out a bottle of scotch from a cupboard, slid two glasses on the counter.

My husband never shows up this time of the day, she said. Her fat fingers stroked her hair.

◎ ◎ ◎

At the motel, breakfast time was already over. There were no cars in the parking lot, but two old men sat in the reception area. The receptionist was a new guy I didn't recognize.

Their monthly rate was much better, so I decided I'd stay for a month.

In my room, I opened my knapsack and spread everything out on the floor. I hadn't organized the objects inside the knapsack in a long time. I undressed and folded my clothes, put them on the flowery bed cover. My underwear I took with me to the bathroom.

The water was leaking from the shower. It had formed a brown stain on the tiles. On the floor, ants were crawling on something sticky.

The water was lukewarm. I thought about going and complaining about it, but didn't want to leave the room with my hair wet. I washed my underwear and spread it on the radiator to dry.

When I was a kid my mother would spread all of my clothes on the radiator before I left home. In my walk to school, I would be warm from the heat until I got very close.

I dried myself with a towel and looked at the mirror. My beard had grown. I first cut it short with a scissor, then shaved it. The skin beneath my beard had become flaky.

One Summer Lily's grandparents came to visit them. They stayed in the farm house for a week. They had their meals together again, her grandmother cooking. Her grandfather said grace. Her father never said grace after her mother was gone. The sound of forks and coughs were the only things that broke the silence.

Her father smoked one cigarette after another.

Her grandparents took her on a camping trip one day. Her father didn't go with them. They swam in the lake, slept in a tent. They showed her birds, chipmunks, deer drinking water from the lake. By the fire pit, her grandmother told stories.

The day after, her grandfather fished and they took a photo with him holding the fish, her grandmother holding Lily. Lily didn't like to touch the fish. It was still alive, moving in her grandfather's hand.

Her grandfather gave her a map where it showed there was a treasure under a tree. The trees all looked alike, she couldn't tell which was which. But that tree seemed closer to the lake. She started digging. There was a box with a black velvet cover that she opened. Two ear rings were inside.

She looked around, but couldn't find her grandparents or the blue tent. The sun had gone down. The wind shook the trees. She heard the branches of the trees crack and fall down. She started screaming.

Her grandparents appeared from behind the trees.

We're here. We're here, they said.

On their way back, they asked her if she wanted to go live with them.

I pictured little Lily with ear rings on.

I tried to remember when I had written this in my notebook.

When I woke up the room was dark. My penis was hard. I didn't remember what I had dreamed. I turned on the lights and checked my underwear on the radiator, it was still damp. I needed to get dressed and go out to eat. I thought I should have at least bought some bread to keep in my room.

I heard a knock at the door. I put on my pants without underpants. When I opened the door, it was the police man from this morning.

Would you mind moving your car? That spot is mine.

I don't have a car.

Sorry about that, he said. His eyes moved on what was inside, on the floor.

Do you happen to have a wrench? the policeman asked. My shower is leaking. I've asked the reception several times, and they haven't done anything about it. I can't go to sleep at night.

I could see his pistol hanging from his belt.

I left the door half open, grabbed the wrench from the floor, gave it to him.

He held it like that for a moment, looking at me, and then he thanked me and left.

◎ ◎ ◎

In the morning, I wore my clothes, organized the items on the floor. I left my tools on the bedside table, put everything else back in the knapsack.

In the reception area, the policeman was having his scrambled eggs with coffee. His pistol was placed on the table. He waved his hand at me as I entered.

The leak is fixed, he said.

Great.

I wanted to have breakfast first, but I decided I'd make my phone call until the police man was gone. I wanted to eat breakfast alone.

I dialled Lily's number with no success again, then returned and sat for breakfast. Both the receptionist and the police officer had their eyes on me.

Pretty nice out there, the receptionist said.

The police man stretched his arm towards me. Jake, he said.

The receptionist was looking at us. He had seen my ID.

I told the police man my real name.

He contorted his face. I'll call you Neighbour, he said and pressed my hand. His knuckles were fat. My hand started to hurt.

What do you do, Neighbour?

I am in between jobs was what I always responded with, even though I hadn't really looked for a new job for several years.

He stood up, reattached his belt, looked into my eyes. His eyes still looked red.

Bye, Neighbour.

After breakfast, I walked back to the other part of the city. I needed to rent a post box at the post office and go back to the ministry to change my address. Instead, I found myself in front of the blue house.

I stepped back from the building and tried to see if I could see anything through the windows. I could see shadows moving inside, so I went closer and knocked.

An old woman opened the door.

I am not buying anything, the woman said with a high-pitched voice.

I am not here to sell anything, I said. I am a friend of the two women living on the top floor.

I had only rented it to one person. A woman with short hair and glasses. They should've paid more if there were two of them. Anyway, she hasn't paid her rent. She disappeared last month. I have rented the place to someone else. Her furniture is in storage. Let her know if you see her.

What had happened to Sheila? She didn't seem like someone who would leave like that.

Can I leave my address with you to give it to her in case she comes back? I am staying at a motel.

I ripped a page out of my notebook and wrote down the name of the motel.

You seem like a nice person, she said. I'll tell you what I heard from a neighbour. Two weeks ago, a woman was screaming and knocking at different doors asking people to help her. She thought somebody was following her. I was out buying groceries, so I didn't see any of this, but when I came back people were still on the street. You could hear the sirens of the ambulance. It might have been her. As I remember, her sound moving upstairs stopped that same night.

Could it be Lily? Lily had talked about people following her with Sheila before I left. Or was it Sheila?

I walked to the post office before going back to the motel. In the post office, I saw the date on a calendar on the wall. On that winter day, in the past, I had moved a few pieces of furniture into the house that belonged to a friend of mine who had just fled the country. The big vacant house was only heated with a rusted oil stove. I couldn't heat the room before going to the hospital to get to Ava. I had to leave the house with the furniture not arranged but on the floor, the stove humming but not emitting heat. I wasn't able to get to the hospital in time.

Ava's high blood pressure had necessitated a C-section. I imagined she'd waited until the very last moment for me. I pictured her looking to the door for a long time, her eyelids heavy from the anaesthetics.

Her face was swollen and tired. But the moment she opened her eyes and saw me holding our son, she smiled.

Our son was very tiny, wrapped around in a grey blanket, fuzzy hair covering his soft skull.

Back at the motel, the air smelled of a dead skunk. The policeman had put a chair on the porch. He puffed at a joint, a beer bottle in his hand.

Join me Neighbour, he said.

Maybe he is not a bad person, I thought.

After two puffs, his husky voice echoed in my head. His face stretched and turned into other faces.

I killed someone today, the policeman said. He started to sob.

I looked at him and pictured him pointing his pistol at his own temple.

First I thought he was the contact, but then he had the policeman's face. We were on my father's boat fishing from the river. I heard his husky voice from beneath the water, his words bubbling out of the surface. I pulled out my fishing rod. His head started to come out of the water. His eyes were shut. The hook stuck out of his gums.

Next morning, I woke up earlier to have my breakfast before the policeman was up. I wasn't ready to face him again this soon. When I saw through the window that he was in the reception area, I started to walk away. First, I had no place in mind, but then I decided to go the place that was a pub before.

When I got there, the woman was dozing with her head on the counter. She raised her head and looked at me. She had sleep marks on her forehead and one of her cheeks.

I am not a morning person. Now that I am selling coffee, I have to wake up early, and no one even wants coffee in this neighbourhood. You're my only customer.

I didn't know if I should be flattered or not. I sat on my stool without swerving.

Were you able to call your friend?

How did you know? I asked. No, it's very weird. It's as if she has disappeared.

Your girlfriend?

No, but someone I was close with.

The things I've seen in my life. Her hazel eyes went absent like the last time. I would check the hospitals, she said as she poured a shot of scotch into my coffee mug.

There were four hospitals in the area. It wasn't possible to tell from the map what departments each of them had, and if they were the right place to look. First, I had to visit all the four hospitals in person.

The problem was that I didn't know Lily and Sheila's last names, not to mention that I wasn't sure which one of them I was looking for. Every time I described the incident at one of the hospitals, they asked me for the patient's last name and my relationship to her.

At the first hospital, which was closer to Lily's blue house, the psych ward was on the sixth floor. Every day, only during the visiting hours, from 12 to 2 pm, the elevator could take you to the psych floor. The elevator's door opened to a big hall with a reception desk where you had to sign your name after your ID was checked. Two security guards searched the visitors after that. From the hallway, you could see some of the patients in their hospital gowns smoking on the balcony, shaking in the cold. They all had white bands on their wrists.

I knew both Sheila and Lily smoked, so I thought if I could wait there for a while I might be able to see them. The problem was you couldn't wait there for a long time with the security guards there.

I went there two days in a row, but had to return down with the elevator as soon as one of the security guards noticed me.

The second time I was walking out of the hospital, somebody called me. I first went faster, but when I turned I saw the orderly that had been with me on the elevator. He had a long face and a shaved head.

When I stopped, he stopped and took a cigarette from behind his ear.

Are you looking for pills?

Pills? No.

It's cool. Don't worry. I can find whatever you need.

I didn't understand why he had mistaken me for an addict, but maybe he was someone I could work with.

I'm looking for a friend of mine who might be a patient here.

I can find her for you. For two hundred. I'll need a hundred ahead though.

I gave him the bill, described all I knew: patient's address, first name (for both Lily and Sheila), and description of both of their appearances.

He told me that he'd meet me tomorrow morning at a coffee shop across the street.

After Lily graduated, she painted, worked temporary jobs in which she didn't last for that long. After a while, she wasn't even painting. Every time she went back to her studio, she stared at her brushes, her old paintings. Once she pushed herself to build a new frame, stretching canvas on it. But after she placed different paints on her palette, she could only stare at the white canvas in front of her.

She thought about finding her mother.

In the coffee shop, the orderly was wearing jeans and a black winter jacket, a black hat on his bald head.

I have what you need, he said. Give me the rest of the money please. He put a piece of paper on the table.

I handed him the bill, flipped the paper. On the paper were Sheila's last name, submission details, and room number.

The orderly gave me his phone number on another scrap of paper. Call me if you need pills, he said.

It was still three hours left to the visiting time. I sat there in the coffee shop, reading through my notes.

Instead of finding her mother, Lily registered in a program where they sent her to a farm for work. They gave her food and a place to sleep in compensation for her labour.

What had made Lily want to go back to the world of farms and barns? For a full page, she'd described how she milked a cow. I'd felt like being in the barn with her. The smell of wet hay, the heat of the animal bodies in the cold air of the morning.

She stayed with an old man and woman on this small farm. They reminded her of her grandparents, gave her a room that had belonged to their daughter. All the photos of the girl were from her childhood, the sheets on her bed had pictures of animals on them. There was nothing else in the room except an empty shelf where Lily put her books.

She had to wake up at 4 am every morning. She was tired like she had never been in her life, and didn't have much time to do anything else, but sometimes she'd draw the animals in the barn when she couldn't go to sleep.

In the house, the wind always rattled the windows. They boiled potatoes, carrots, and peas for dinner on the wood stove. The old man mashed the potatoes on the kitchen table with the back of a spoon, adding milk, butter, dried thyme he gathered from the mountain.

After the harvest, the old man killed a goat. They roasted the goat, had it with mashed potatoes, with wine the man had made years ago from the grapes of their own vines.

The old man sometimes called her Jane.

Lily assumed Jane was the name of the daughter. She never asked about it.

I took the elevator to the sixth floor and provided the person at the reception with Sheila's full name and room number. They checked my ID, and I signed in my name on a piece of paper. They put my knapsack on a shelf and searched all of my pockets.

In the room, Sheila was lying on the bed with her eyes closed. She was pale and had lost some weight. Her hair had grown longer. I wasn't used to seeing her without her glasses and with the long hair.

She sleeps for most of the day, the old woman on the bed beside her said. It's all the drugs.

I had only two hours until the visiting time was over, so I wondered if I should wake her. When I touched her arm, she jerked her body.

Don't worry, Sheila. I patted her arm.

What're you doing here?

I'm here to see you.

She started to cry and to shake. I don't feel so well, she kept repeating.

What happened?

I don't know. I wasn't feeling so well, and then I started to feel really bad.

I didn't say anything to this.

By the way, Lily came back, and looked for you, but she left again.

Yes, she did, Bob. I know you're not here for me, but for her. But she's gone. Like always. When people need her.

I was worried about you too, I said.

Her bed was by the window side. You could see the bare trees through the window. She noticed me looking out at the trees.

Do you see that plastic bag on the tree? Sheila said.

I nodded.

It has been there from the day I came here.

A nurse came in with the cart of food. She pushed the cart of food beside Sheila's bed. On her plate, there were boiled vegetables, a grilled chicken breast.

The chicken tastes like rubber here, Sheila said. She pressed the plastic knife on the chicken until the knife broke into two pieces.

She needs to rest now, the nurse said, and directed me towards the door.

I'll see you tomorrow, I said to Sheila.

In the hallway, a young boy was screaming. His mouth foamed. The orderly and one of the security guards were holding him down. Another nurse ran towards them and injected the boy with a syringe.

The orderly turned towards me and winked.

Next day I bought two cheeseburgers before going back to the hospital.

Sheila ate with more appetite. She told me about her day, about people at her group therapy sessions. She held my hand as she was talking.

What did you talk about today? I asked.

Sheila's father had gone bankrupt when she was thirteen. He was arrested one day when she was at school. They had to move to a different neighborhood where they could afford the rent.

It was the middle of a school year, so she couldn't change her school. Her mother paid their past driver to drive her to school.

Sheila didn't explain how her family could afford the driver but not the rent.

Her aunt had given her mother one of her cousin's dresses. Her cousin went to the same school, was two grades ahead of Sheila. One day in the school yard, her cousin saw Sheila wearing the dress and asked her about it. Her cousin didn't know that her mother had given Sheila the dress.

The driver was the only connection to Sheila's past life. As they drove every morning, the landscape shifted from deserted industrial buildings and red brick towers to upscale houses with porches and plants.

She remembered the driver smelling of cigarettes and cologne. His big strong hands, she said.

After she said this, she started to cry.

I had pimples on my face, Sheila said. We were poor. No boy my age liked me.

She went silent and stared at the plastic bag on the tree.

Do you want to talk about it more?

No.

I stood beside her bed, caressing her face. She squeezed on the edge of the bed and wrapped her right arm around my waist. She pressed her face on my belly, her tears wetting my shirt. I started to shiver.

The nurse came in and gave me a look that told me I had to leave.

◎ ◎ ◎

I walked to the woman's place that used to be a pub. When I got there the door was closed. Cardboards were placed behind the windows. "FOR LEASE," was hand-written with a red marker on a piece of paper between the cardboard and the glass.

On my way back to the motel, I stood on the bridge and looked at the frozen river. I could still hear water whispering beneath the sheets of ice.

Out of the fingerless glove, my fingers burned from the cold and became numb. I put my hands in the pockets of my khaki jacket. The gloves were one of the few things from Ava that I kept. A lot of fun was made about my hands being as small as hers.

I took my son with me to buy her these gloves for her birthday. The night that we gave her the gloves we were in front of the restaurant where I'd made a reservation. We usually didn't eat out, or even when we did we didn't go to such places. That was a special night.

When we got out of the restaurant, Ava put the gloves on. I looked at her fingers, at my son's eyes staring at his mother's hands. I envied those eyes.

Before we went to the restaurant, I had arrived home and hidden the cake in the mechanical room. When we returned, the cake had melted in the box. The sides of the box were smeared.

We were too happy to care.

◎ ◎ ◎

In the motel room, I held my head in my hands.

◎ ◎ ◎

I woke to the sound of the policeman knocking at the door.
When I opened the door, he grabbed the collar of my shirt
and pulled me outside.

I had difficulty breathing and started to cough.

Are you running away from me? Forget whatever I told
you. Do you understand? If you tell anyone anything, you
know what will happen.

Yes. Yes. I understand.

His eyes were red again. He looked at me, exhaled deeply,
and left.

If you follow them, you won't get lost.

I decided I'll mail the pilot certificate back to the French man's address. I hadn't noticed anyone following me after I had returned from the water treatment plant. I didn't want to give those people any excuses.

The problem with the policeman was something easier.

As for Sheila, she might have still required my presence. But I wasn't sure. My damage might have been more given her vulnerable situation.

As I was walking to the post office, I found myself thinking about what Sheila had told me yesterday, what had happened to her then.

Despite what had happened in her childhood, she'd seemed fine the first time I met her. At the time, I had only thought about myself, about Lily. I thought about the night that I had seen her feet beneath the velvet curtain.

I didn't even know what she used to do for a living.

I thought I'll go see her again after going to the post office.

Why had Lily left us alone like this?

◎ ◎ ◎

In the post office after mailing the pilot certificate, I opened my post box to get rid of the junk mail. The only thing I found in the post box was a photo of two red-crowned cranes dancing on the snow. They had opened their wings, tilted their heads towards the sky. Their black beak and legs and their red crowns separated them from the white background. It was as if they were praying.

Each year my dad would take me on his boat when the white cranes migrated. Each year there were fewer and fewer.

On the back of the photo there was a stamp with a painting of cherry blossoms.

From Lily, For Bob, was written below the stamp.

Lily probably didn't know about her lost notebook yet.

I wished there had been an address on the back of the photo. I could have sent Lily a letter, give her one of my own notebooks.

I tried to understand how Lily had found my post box address. Insofar as I knew, only the ministry of labour had my address.

If Lily had been able to find it without knowing my real name from somewhere else, there was no reason that others couldn't.

For a moment, I wondered whether Lily was actually in town.

I had given Sheila's landlord the name of my motel. This could have been not such a great idea.

I turned around and looked at the sidewalk, at the cars parked beside the curbs, the passengers sitting inside. In the front seat of an old blue truck, a man was asleep with his head on the steering wheel.

I waited there for him to raise his head. I walked around the truck. There was nothing strange. The windshield had a crack on it. Inside the car, there were coffee cups, banana peels.

I waited there for a while and the man didn't raise his head.

I tried to imagine Sheila's past jobs: librarian, lab technician, cook, graphic designer.

I couldn't think of anything else. The first time I had met her, the precision in her movements had attracted my attention. She had been so different from the Sheila I'd seen in the hospital.

Sometimes people hid themselves behind what they wanted others to see.

I hadn't gone to the market in years. The market was another place where you could watch the lobsters. Here, they kept them in big fish tanks. The lobsters had more space to move here, but their claws were tied, tired.

On a week day, the market would not be crowded. There were very few people, on their lunch breaks, sitting on benches, biting at their lobster sandwiches.

There were two stalls that sold jewellery. I bought Sheila a pair of ear rings. They had two little yellow stones hanging from them.

I checked the time, and I realized I was too late for the visiting hour at the hospital.

I'll go visit Sheila tomorrow, I thought.

◎ ◎ ◎

After the market, I went to the library and searched the news for anything new about the death of the contact.

When I couldn't find anything about it, I sat behind a desk and browsed a book about lobsters.

◎ ◎ ◎

Lobsters mate after the female molts. Before that stage the female releases pheromones into the water to let nearby males know she is preparing to molt and mate. If there are multiple males interested in the female, they will fight each other for her. The lobster that wins the fight will take the female into his cave and protect her from predators. The male turns her over gently and pierces her abdomen with his first pair of pleodods.

In my dream, Sheila was lying on the snow. Her eyes were closed. She had long hair that reached to her feet. The red-crowned cranes were dancing around her body. They started to peck at her pale skin.

The next morning, I left the motel room without having breakfast. The policeman's car wasn't in the parking lot. It was a sunny day, and the snow was now slush. As I walked, I heard the sound of a car's tires splashing slush behind me. I turned back and I saw a black car turn into an alley.

◎ ◎ ◎

In the hospital, when I provided the patient's name for my visit, they told me I can't visit Sheila. She was transferred to the locked ward was what they said.

When I asked the nurse when I could visit her, she told me she didn't know.

Can you give her these? I gave the nurse the ear rings.

She took them, rolled her eyes, and started talking to other nurses.

I wished I had showed up yesterday, or from the very beginning hadn't showed up in Sheila's life.

I went to the first floor and dialled the number that the orderly had given me. I left him a voice message.

◎ ◎ ◎

The wind moved the bare trees in the hospital yard. I looked and looked, but couldn't find the plastic bag on the limbs of the trees.

An old woman on her wheelchair grabbed a cigarette butt from the ground and started to smoke it.

What are you looking at? She asked me.

Can you find my cat? she asked me. It hasn't returned home.

Aren't you in the army? she said. My husband is in the army. He hasn't sent me any letters in a while.

I felt too tired to walk back to the motel, so I got on the bus.

◎ ◎ ◎

In the bus, I wondered where Lily was. I tried to remember her face. After all, I had only seen her the once. Did I even remember her the way she really looked?

How did the things written in her diary relate to her face, to her body? Hadn't I reconstructed her in my head after reading the diary?

But what if she hadn't even written it? What if that phone number I had called hadn't been Lily's phone number? Sheila might have just got a voice message from a stranger, decided to call back.

There was first the loud sound of a bullet punching a hole through the window. I was out of the shower, getting ready for bed.

As I ducked, I heard the shattering of glass, the policeman screaming, another shooting closer to me. I raised my head, saw the black car accelerating away.

I had to put on shoes to walk through the shattered glass.

In the next room, the policeman had fallen on the floor. A bone poked out of his right shoulder. His blood black on the carpet. He kept screaming.

I could hear sirens. Soon a crowd gathered there.

The policeman used to work for the narcotics department.

All the notebooks were gathered as scene evidence. I don't think anybody tried to read them, but they weren't returned to me.

In my new room, I have a desk. The back of my chair faces the window. I hear the wind rustling the leaves of the trees. My head turns but I do not see a plastic bag.

No cars are on the street. I have the photo of the red-crowned cranes above my desk.

Acknowledgments

I would like to thank Peter Markus for his suggestions, his words, and his writing. This book would have not existed without him.

I am grateful to Zach Davidson for his comradeship, his reading of my work over the years and our long conversations around writing and books.

Finally, thanks to Giancarlo DiTrapano for believing in this book and making it happen.